Edgar Badger's
Butterfly
Day

Edgar Badger's Butterfly Day

by Monica Kulling

illustrated by **Neecy Twinem**

For Bobbi Katz—M.K.

With love for Vincent—N.T.

Text copyright © 1999 by Monica Kulling
Illustrations copyright © 1999 by Neecy Twinem

For information contact:
MONDO Publishing
One Plaza Road
Greenvale, New York 11548

Visit our web site at http://www.mondopub.com

Designed by Eliza Green
Production by The Kids at Our House

Printed in Hong Kong
99 00 01 02 03 04 05 06   9 8 7 6 5 4 3 2 1

Library of Congress Cataloging-in-Publication Data
Kulling, Monica.
    Edgar Badger's butterfly day / by Monica Kulling ; illustrated by Neecy
Twinem.
        p.   cm.
    Summary: Because he's sad and can't face the end of summer, Edgar
Badger escapes by going to bed and staying there until his friends come
around to cheer him up.
    ISBN 1-57255-604-8 (pbk. : alk. paper)
    [1. Emotions—Fiction. 2. Autumn—Fiction. 3. Friendship—Fiction.]
I. Twinem, Neecy, ill. II. Title.
PZ7.K9490155Eg   1999
[E]—dc21   98-3206
                                                              CIP
                                                              AC

Contents

Goodbye Summer

It was autumn. The days were warm. The nights were cool. And the leaves were falling.

Edgar Badger stood in his garden.

He held a rake in one paw. He held

a hoe in the other paw.

"Goodbye summer," he sighed.

"Goodbye garden."

Edgar's neighbors loved his garden.

Duncan Bear was crazy about the
tomatoes.

"I've never tasted a tastier tomato,"
Duncan said. Tomato juice ran down
his furry chin.

Henry Raccoon loved the lettuce. "There's no better lettuce anywhere," said Henry. He could chomp through a whole head in seconds.

Even Violet Porcupine praised Edgar's garden.

"It's a snap to love these beans," she said, crunching happily. "Edgar, you are the best gardener in these woods."

Edgar sighed again.

"Winter is in the air," he said. "It's
time to put my garden to bed."

But Edgar didn't want to let summer
go. He couldn't face it. So *he* went to
bed instead. He crawled under the
covers and pulled them over his head.

Picking Apples

The next morning, Duncan knocked on Edgar's door. The door swung open. "Anybody home?" Duncan called. No answer.

Duncan peeked into the bedroom. He found Edgar in bed.

"Still in bed?" Duncan asked. "I can't believe it. It's nearly lunchtime."

Edgar poked his nose out from under
the covers.

"Summer came and summer went,"
he said. "And I am sad to see it gone."

"But it's a crackerjack day," said Duncan.
"The apples are red and ripe. Let's go pick
a basketful."

Duncan loved autumn apples. He could
eat them all day long.

17

Slowly Edgar pulled himself out of bed.

He put on his jacket and followed

Duncan into the forest.

The trees were full of apples.

"The ripest ones are at the top," said Duncan. "I'm big and strong. I'll scoot up this tree and shake the apples down. Then you can pick them up."

That doesn't sound like much fun, thought Edgar. But he didn't say anything. He didn't want to disappoint Duncan.

Duncan was a heavy bear. He wasn't
the best at scooting. It took him a
little time to climb the tree.
This is boring, thought Edgar.

Edgar left Duncan in the tree. He
walked home and went back to bed.

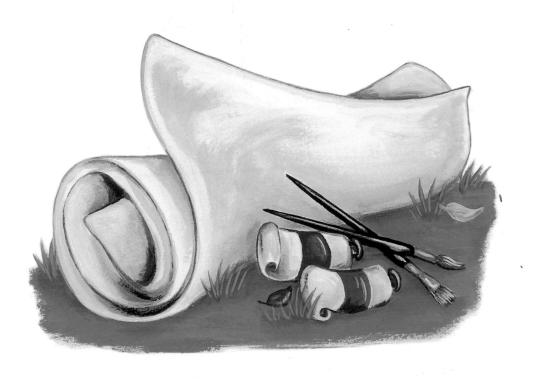

Watching Paint Dry

After lunch, Henry went to visit Edgar.
He found Edgar's door wide open.
"What's this?" said Henry. "Are you
here, Edgar?"
No answer.

Henry walked into Edgar's house.
He looked in the bedroom. Edgar
was still in bed.
"Taking an afternoon nap?" Henry
asked.

Edgar poked his nose out from under
the covers.

"Summer came and summer went,"
he sighed. "And I am very sad to see
it gone."

"But the day is full of color," said Henry.
"The leaves are yellow and orange and
red. Come paint a picture of the forest
with me."

Edgar felt too blue to paint. But he
didn't want to disappoint Henry. So
he got out of bed and put on his jacket.

Edgar followed Henry into the forest. A
large piece of paper lay on the ground.
"I put down the first coat of paint," said
Henry. "We have to wait for it to dry.
Then we can paint on it."

Edgar and Henry waited. And waited.

And waited some more.

This is boring, thought Edgar.

Henry seemed to like watching the paint dry. He didn't take his eyes off the paper. So he didn't see Edgar leave for home.

Counting Butterflies

At suppertime, Violet knocked on
Edgar's door.
No answer.

Violet opened the door. She peeked into the bedroom. There was Edgar lying in bed.

"Taking a suppertime snooze?" asked Violet.

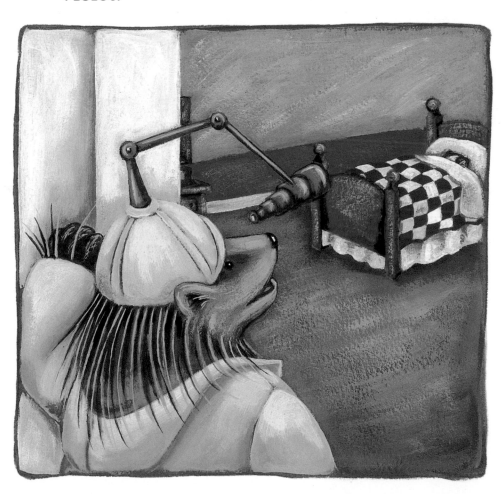

Edgar poked his nose out from under
the covers.

"Summer came and summer went," he
said. "And I am oh so sad to see it gone."

Edgar was tired of saying the same thing over and over again. He was so tired he was glad he was in bed.

"But the butterflies are flying at dawn," said Violet. "They are napping in the trees right now. I can see them with my telescope!"

Edgar had made Violet a hat with a telescope on it. She was always cheerful when she wore it.

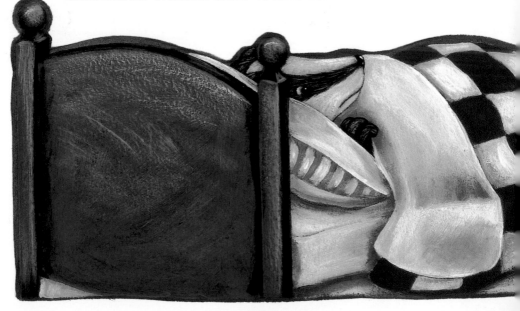

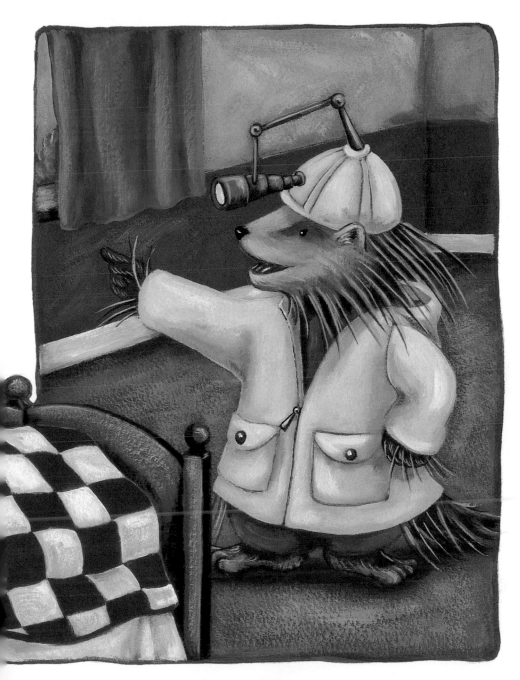

"Come count butterflies with me," urged Violet.

Count butterflies! What will they think of next? thought Edgar.

Instead of getting out of bed, Edgar shook his head. He was sorry to disappoint Violet, but he was not moving.

Violet left to count butterflies by herself.

A Butterfly Surprise

*T*he next day Edgar stayed in bed all day. His friends were getting worried. One-by-one they dropped by to cheer him up.

"Smell this apple," said Duncan. He
stuck an apple under Edgar's nose.
The apple smelled of autumn leaves
and mountain streams.
Edgar took a tiny bite of the apple.
"Delicious," he said. But still Edgar
did not get out of bed.

Henry came by.

"Here's my painting of the forest,"
he said.

Henry's forest looked more alive than
any forest Edgar had seen. But it did
not make Edgar want to get out of bed.

Violet came by with a butterfly in a jar. The butterfly had orange and black wings.

Violet opened the jar.

"Surprise!" she exclaimed.

The butterfly flew into the room.

It floated above Edgar.

"What a wonder," Edgar murmured.

He sat up.

"It has beautiful colors," agreed Henry.

"It's so tiny and light," said Duncan.

Violet went to the open window. Edgar
got out of bed. He watched the butterfly
sail into the autumn sunshine.

"What a golden day," said Edgar.

Then Edgar noticed his garden.

"My garden sure could use some work,"
he said. "I better get to it right away."

Edgar got dressed and waddled out to his garden. His friends went with him. They helped Edgar put his garden to bed.

"How wonderful autumn is," said Edgar.

"I am glad to see it here."